THE CHILDREN OF CHELM

by *David A. Adler*
illustrated by *Arthur Friedman*

BONIM BOOKS

New York • London

To My Parents, With Love
D.A.

Library of Congress Cataloging in Publication Data

Adler, David A
   The children of Chelm.

   SUMMARY: Three stories from the fictional Polish town of
Chelm where the "wise" council members, though doing their
best, make foolish decisions regarding the townspeople.
   [1. Jews in Poland—Fiction.   2. Humorous stories]
I. Friedman, Arthur, 1935-   II. Title.
PZ7.A2615Ch   [E]   79-20617
ISBN 0-88482-722-0
ISBN 0-88482-773-9 pbk.

BONIM BOOKS

A division of Hebrew Publishing Company
80 Fifth Avenue
New York, N.Y. 10011

Printed in the United States of America

CONTENTS

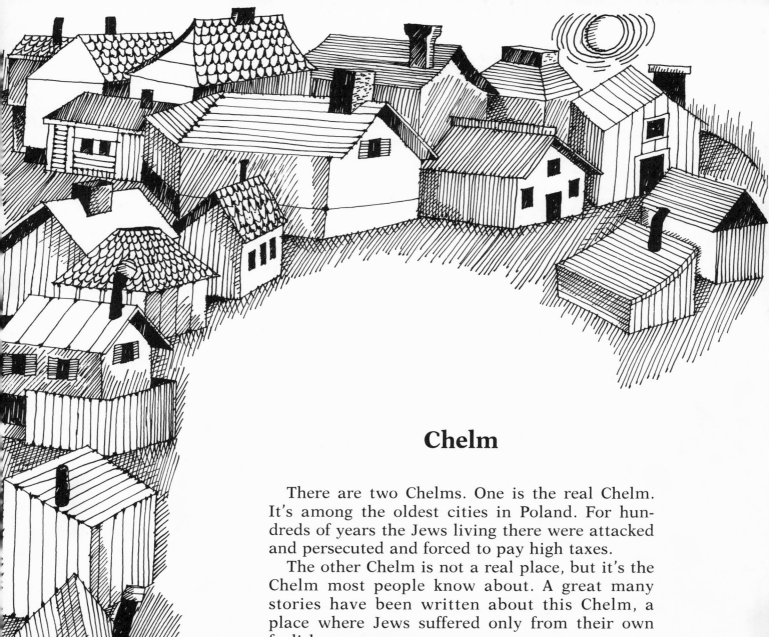

Chelm

There are two Chelms. One is the real Chelm. It's among the oldest cities in Poland. For hundreds of years the Jews living there were attacked and persecuted and forced to pay high taxes.

The other Chelm is not a real place, but it's the Chelm most people know about. A great many stories have been written about this Chelm, a place where Jews suffered only from their own foolishness.

The stories of Chelm were told during some very dark times in our history. Hopefully they gave the Jews of the real Chelm and elsewhere a reason to smile.

THE CHILDREN AND THEIR BATHS

In Chelm the Sabbath was a day of rest. But Friday wasn't. On Friday men, women and children rushed to prepare for the Sabbath. They baked and cooked and cleaned.

For the children Friday was also bath day. There were no large tubs or empty barrels in Chelm, so the children bathed in the river.

"I hate this water," the children would yell. "It's cold."

"Mommy, Mommy, I stepped on a frog."

"It's starting to rain. I'm getting wet."

As the weeks passed, the children yelled louder and louder until one day the noise was so great a whole regiment of soldiers thought a war had begun in Chelm and marched into the city.

The soldiers looked for someone to fight. They ran through the muddy streets of Chelm. They threw open doors. But all they found were men and women preparing for the Sabbath. They ran to the river. But all they found there were the children.

9

After the soldiers left, Sender the Shoemaker gathered all the parents and their children. He led them to the small one-room house where the Wise Council of Chelm sat.

"What can we do?" Sender asked. "Our children hate to bathe, but they must be clean for the Sabbath."

"Hmmm," said one council member, "why not have the children take shorter baths?"

"No," another member said, "let them take dry baths. They'll go to the edge of the river but not in. Then they won't be cold or step on frogs."

"Fool!" a third council member called out. "If they don't get wet, how will they dry themselves!"

The council members argued for a full seven days and seven nights. All during that time Berel, the wisest of them all, was thinking, counting on his fingers and writing numbers on a sheet of paper. Suddenly he jumped up.

"I've got it!" he yelled. "I've studied the numbers and I've figured it out.

"Even a fool knows that you can save gold coins one at a time or find a purse filled with them. If you save fifty or find fifty it's all the same. Fifty is fifty.

"It's no different with baths. Our children don't have to take their baths one at a time. Let them take a whole year's worth all at once."

12

And that's what they did.

Once each year the children bathed in the river.
They took fifty short baths one right after the
other. They still didn't like to bathe, but since it
was only once a year, and since each bath was
very, very short, the children didn't complain.

THE DAY IT SNOWED

The city of Chelm was seldom beautiful. The roads were often muddy. The houses were old and needed paint. And whenever a flower grew in Chelm, a hungry goat came and ate it.

But one day Chelm was beautiful, the day it snowed.

The snow began as a light flurry. Then large flakes fell to the ground. Soon a beautiful white blanket had covered the city.

It was a member of Chelm's Wise Council who
first noticed the snow.

"Look," he said. "Snow has covered my roof.
Now I won't have to patch up the leak. The snow
will keep the water out."

16

"And we don't have to fix the roads," another
member said. "The snow has made them all level
and smooth."

"But the people of Chelm must all stay where they are," Berel, the wisest member announced. "If they walk outside, the smooth beautiful snow will be ruined."

"He's right."

"Footprints ruin snow."

"Berel is always right."

18

Berel smiled. "First," he said, "we must send a messenger to every house in Chelm. He'll tell our people to stay where they are."

"But what about the children?" someone asked.
"They can't stay in school overnight."

The council members began to argue.

"No one can be allowed to walk in the snow. Not even the children."

"At night children belong at home."

"But they can't walk outside. We mustn't have footprints."

"Well they can't stay in school. The school has no beds."

"Enough!" Berel yelled. "You're all fools," he said. "Of course the children must go home, and of course they must not step in the snow."

"But how can they go home and not step in the snow?" one member of the Wise Council asked.

Berel smiled. "The answer is so simple. We'll go to the school, put the children on our shoulders and carry them home."

And that's what they did.

Of course, when the wise men returned to their council room and looked out the window they saw a great many footprints in the snow. But even as they took off their wet shoes they had no idea who had disobeyed their edict and walked in the snow.

A NEW SCHOOL FOR CHELM

The school in Chelm was old and too small.
Many of the children had to learn standing up.

"We need a new school," someone said at a meeting of the Wise Council."

"When it rains, the roof leaks. My child's head gets wet," someone else said.

"It's so crowded," the teacher told the council, "each child knows what the other is thinking. I can't give any tests."

"Well," Berel announced, "if we need a new school, we'll build one. And since this is Chelm, it will be the best school ever built."

Early the next morning everyone in Chelm went to the top of a nearby mountain. There were hundreds of large stones on the top of the mountain. The people planned to shape the stones and use them to build the walls of the new school.

Each stone was so heavy, it took four people to
carry it down the mountain.

The children watched as the stones were carried down. Then, when almost all the stones were at the base of the mountain, one little girl pulled at Berel's sleeve.

29

"That's not very smart," the girl said.

"What isn't smart?"

"It's not smart to carry all those big stones down the mountain. No one lives at the base of the mountain. It would be much easier just to push the stones and let them roll down."

"Hmm," Berel said, "you're right."

Berel ran down the mountain. "Carry all those stones back up," he told the workers. "I'm going to make the work easy for you. When you get the stones to the top of the mountain just push them and let them roll down."

And that's what they did.
It was hard work carrying those heavy stones
back up the mountain. But pushing them down
was almost no work at all.

Copy 2

E
ADL   Adler, David A.
        The children of
        Chelm

Date Due